For Christiane

First published in Great Britain in 2004
By Zero To Ten, part of Evans Publishing Group
2A Portman Mansions
Chiltern Street
London W1U 6NR

© 2002 l'école des loisirs, Paris
Translation © 2004 by Su Swallow

British Library Cataloguing in Publication Data
Jadoul, Emile
    Push me higher!
    1. Children's stories - Pictorial works
    I. Title
    843.9'14(J)

ISBN 1 84089 307 9

Printed in China

Émile Jadoul

Push me higher!

ZERO TO TEN

Pig needed to go on the swing.

"I'll help you," said Giraffe.
"Thank you, Giraffe," said Pig.
"Push me high, please!"

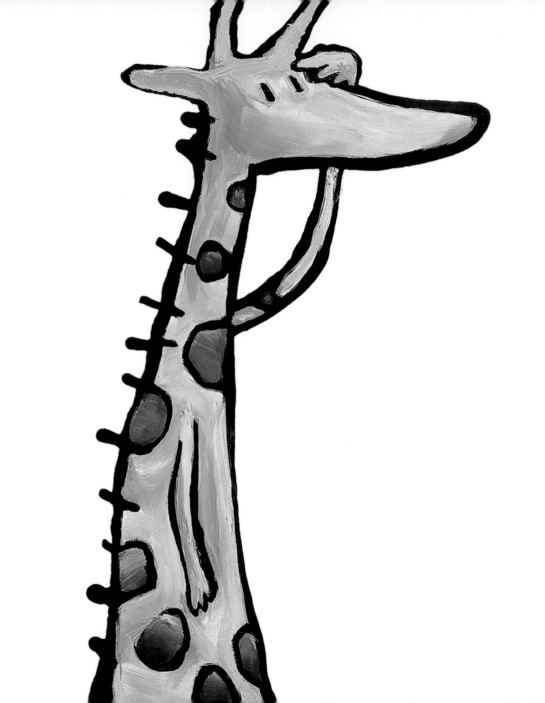

"Push me higher!"

"I'll help you, too," said Rabbit.
"It will be better with
two of us pushing!"

"Thank you, Rabbit," said Pig.
"Push me higher...
and even higher!"

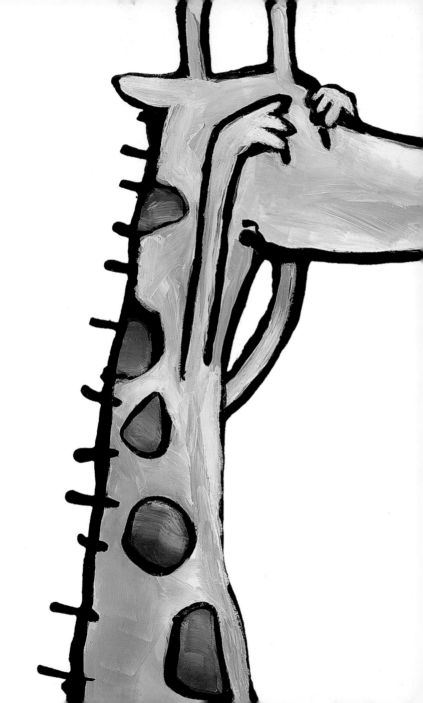

"**Whoops!**" said Rabbit.
"Look out, Pig.
Be careful!" said Giraffe.

"Hello," said Bear.
"I've come to push, too."
"It's even better with
three pushing!"

oOF

"Thank you, Bear," said Pig.
"Push me higher...
and even higher!"

"Just a little bit higher, everyone," shouted Pig. "I'm nearly there!"

"One more push..."

"Wheeeeeeee

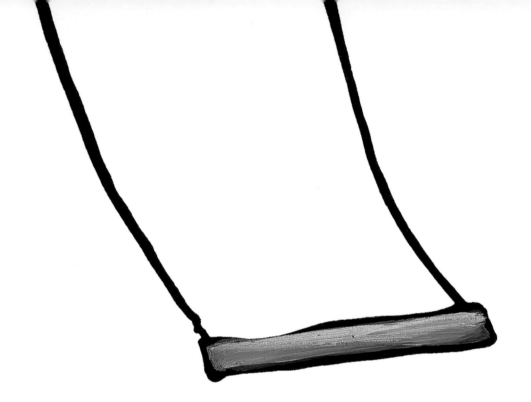

"Made it!"